QUACKER MEETS CANADIAN GOOSE

4

5

This book is dedicated to...
children all over the world...
to put smiles on their faces,
joy in their hearts,
and to create food for good thoughts...
...And especially to those children
who have no parents,
for whatever reason,
God loves you and so do we!

Ricky Van Shelton &

May the Good Lord bless you all!

P.S. This book is written by inspiration from above, illustrated by orders from above, and published by grace from above!

NOW QUACKER THE DUCK
WAS WANDERING AROUND
ON THE FARM
WHERE HE WAS AT...

SO HE WADDLED
ON DOWN
TO A NICE COOL POND...

PLUNGED IN
WITH A SPLATTER,
SPLAT, SPLAT!

HE SWAM LIKE A FROG,
AND THEN LIKE A DOG,
AND THEN LIKE A
LITTLE DUCK DO!...

...WHEN ALL OF A SUDDEN
HIS HEAD WAS A-BUTTIN'
A GOOSE WAS
SWIMMING THERE TOO!

"WELL HELLO!" SAID QUACKER,
"HELLO!" SAID GOOSE,
"AND NOW THAT THE HOWDY DO DO'S...

...ARE ALL IN THE PAST!"
HE SAID WITH A LAUGH.
"YOU'RE THE DUCK
THAT MET MRS. MOO!"

"YOU'RE QUITE RIGHT!"
SAID QUACKER
WITH A HONK
AND A QUACK!!!

"I'VE SEEN YOU SOMEWHERE,
MAYBE UP IN THE AIR...
YOU SURE LOOK
FAMILIAR, YOU DO!"

"I LIVE UP NORTH
WHERE IT SNOWS ALOT!
THEY CALL ME
CANADIAN GOOSE."

...BUT I FLY DOWN
TO VISIT
THIS NICE WARM SPOT...

...TO SWIM
IN THE POND
JUST LIKE YOU!"

"CANADIAN GOOSE!
CANADIAN GOOSE!"
QUACKER SAID WITH A GRIN.

"I HAVE A COUSIN
WHO LIVES UP THERE.
COULD YOU POSSIBLY BE HIM?"

"...WELL, LET'S WALK
AND TALK..."
SAID QUACKER THE DUCK,

"...AND SIT UNDER THE BIG OAK TREE..."

"...YOU TELL ME
ABOUT YOU
AND ALL THAT YOU KNOW...

...AND THEN I'LL TELL YOU ABOUT ME!"

SO THEY WADDLED
AND WALKED
AND SQUAWKED AND TALKED...

...BUT FOUND
THAT THEY
WERE NO KIN.

'CAUSE CANADIAN GOOSE
WAS FOUND BY A MOOSE.
A LITTLE ORPHAN GOOSE
HE WAS THEN.

"YOU HAVEN'T A MOTHER
OR FATHER YOU KNOW?"
QUACKER SAID
WITH DELIGHT!

"WELL I'M SURE I DO...
BUT I DON'T KNOW WHO
BUT WHY DO YOU SMILE
AT MY PLIGHT?...

DO YOU THINK IT'S FUNNY
'CAUSE I HAVE NO PARENTS
TO LOVE ME
AND HOLD ME TIGHT?"

"OF COURSE NOT!" SAID QUACKER.
"I'M JUST LIKE YOU,
EXCEPT I HAVE SISTERS
AND BROTHERS.."

"BUT I NEVER KNEW DAD,
AND I KNOW THAT IT'S SAD...
AND I BARELY REMEMBER
MY MOTHER."

I JUST FELT
THAT I WAS THE ONLY ONE
WHO NEVER KNEW
MOM OR DAD...

...BUT NOW THAT I SEE
YOU ARE JUST LIKE ME
IT KIND OF MADE
MY HEART GLAD.

'CAUSE WE'RE KIND OF KIN
IN OUR OWN SPECIAL WAY
TO KNOW THERE'S
LOVE IN THE WORLD...

'CAUSE YOU WOULDN'T BE GOOSE
IF IT WEREN'T FOR A MOOSE.
AND I WOULDN'T BE DUCK
WITHOUT SQUIRREL!

Illustrated by:

Shan Williams
P.O. Box 119
Dowelltown, TN 37059

You may write to Quacker at:

Quacker Fan Club
P.O. Box 121074
Nashville, Tennessee 37212

Also available from Quacker and RVS Books, Inc.:

"Tales From A Duck Named Quacker"
and
"Quacker Meets Mrs. Moo"